# Visiting Ted in Heaven

BY JANET McGEE

ILLUSTRATED BY DEBORAH GARCIA

BEAVER'S POND PRESS

ISBN 13: 978-1-59298-749-8
Library of Congress Catalog Number: 2018944022
Printed in the United States of America
First Printing: 2018
22 21 20 19 18 5 4 3 2 1

My heartfelt thanks to Janet, who allowed me to portray the love she has for her son, Ted. It was an incredible privilege.

—D. A. G.

To learn more about Ted's story, visit:
JanetMcGee.com

BEAVER'S POND PRESS

Beaver's Pond Press
7108 Ohms Lane
Edina, MN 55439–2129
(952) 829-8818
www.BeaversPondPress.com
To order, call (800)-901-3480. Reseller discounts available.

"Blessed are the pure in heart, for they will see God."
Matthew 5:8

Dedicated to my precious son, Ted.

As the medical staff worked to save you that day, I begged God for a miracle. But I've since learned I don't get to demand or define miracles. And I know now that my true miracle had already happened, which was you, blessing my life for twenty-two months. I miss you deeply and I love you beyond words.

Love, Mom

God, thank you for trusting me to raise Your child, Ted, if only for a little while. It was a huge honor.

One night I had a dream
that I visited someone I love very much
in Heaven. His name is Ted.

In my dream, I was driving in the country and saw a deer cross the road.

Shortly after, I saw a brown bear also cross the road.

There were almost twenty brown bears in the field. "Why are there so many animals surrounding me?" I thought.

I kept driving.

Then three moose
crossed the road.

They were huge,
majestic creatures!
I couldn't believe
all of the animals
around me.

Then a fourth moose
started to run toward me.
I was scared he might hit my car!

But the moose only nudged my car into the ditch
and I began gliding over the land.

**Next I saw three polar bears out of the corner of my eye. The season had changed from fall to winter and it was dark outside. I continued to glide across the icy terrain.**

**I viewed the winter night in amazement.**
**Icy trees and mountains surrounded me.**
**Colorful lights soared through the sky.**
**It was beautiful, unlike anything I had ever seen before!**

A tree in the distance was glowing in the winter night. As I approached the tree, I noticed its trunk was on fire and its branches were icy. It was magical!

"I must be in Heaven,"
I thought.
"It's the only place fire and ice
can exist together and
not hurt each other."

**And then it was summer. Lush, green hills and bountiful trees covered the land around me.**

A woman met me at the top of the hill.

**"Am I in Heaven?" I asked.**
**She said, "Yes!"**
**"Can I see someone while I'm here?"**
**"Of course you can," she said.**
**She told me to close my eyes and imagine**
**who I wanted to see, and I would be there.**

I thought of Ted. When I opened my eyes,
I saw many buildings.

**Before I knew it, we were walking into one of the buildings.**
**I noticed a list of names and room numbers written in chalk.**
**We used to love playing with chalk together**
**when Ted lived on Earth with me.**
**The woman told me Ted was in room 6.**

I walked into room 6, and then—

We hugged each other so tightly! It was the first time I'd seen Ted since he died.

I told him how much I love him and miss him, and that his daddy and brothers love and miss him also. Ted said he loves us too, but doesn't understand why we miss him so much because he sees us every day.

It made my heart glad to hear that even though Ted has a new home in Heaven, he is still with us all the time!

Ted told me he has two pets: a cat named
Mr. Bangles and a dog named Boots.
It made me so happy to know he has pets in Heaven.
Ted loved animals when he lived here on Earth.

I noticed a bin full of toys, including one that we put in his casket when he died. He told me that toy is his favorite and he loves playing with it. He thanked me for giving it to him when he died.

**Even though I didn't want to leave, I knew it was time for me to go. I hugged Ted one last time and told him I loved him.**

**He told me it wouldn't be long for him until we see each other again. Time is different in Heaven. What seems like a long time on Earth doesn't seem long in Heaven.**

**As I left, the scenery around me started breaking apart.**

I woke up right away.
My dream showed me how close
I am to Heaven every day.
Sometimes we think Heaven is
very far away, but it is really close
to us here on Earth.

I still miss Ted deeply,
but after my dream,
I know he is with me
every day. He is safe and
happy living in Heaven.
Someday we will be
together again!